SPACE VOYAGE

GALAXY VOYAGE

CATHERINE BARR

Published in 2022 by The Rosen Publishing Group, Inc.
29 East 21st Street, New York, NY 10010

Originally Published in English by Haynes Publishing under the title:
Space Pocket Manual © Catherine Barr 2019

All rights reserved. No part of this book may be reproduced in any form without permission in writing from the publisher, except by a reviewer.

Cataloging-in-Publication Data

Names: Barr, Catherine.
Title: Galaxy voyage / Catherine Barr.
Description: New York : PowerKids Press, 2022. | Series: Space voyage
Identifiers: ISBN 9781725331877 (pbk.) | ISBN 9781725331891 (library bound) | ISBN 9781725331884 (6 pack) | ISBN 9781725331907 (ebook)
Subjects: LCSH: Galaxies--Juvenile literature. | Milky Way--Juvenile literature.
Classification: LCC QB857.3 B365 2022 | DDC 523.1'12--dc23

Design and layout by Richard Parsons

Cover, p. 1 (control panel) Sky vectors/shutterstock.com; cover, p. 1 (background) NASA Images/Shutterstock.com; pp. 6-32 (background), 3, 4-5, 6, 7 (inset), 12-13, 14, 15, 18, 19 (top), 26, 27 (top), 29 (bottom left); pp. 7 (main), 8, 9, 10, 11, 16, 17, 19 (bottom), 20, 21, 22 (both), 23 (both), 24-25 Courtesy of NASA; pp. 27 (bottom), 29 (top right) Alamy; p. 28 (top) https://commons.wikimedia.org/wiki/File:Thomas_Wright_(astronomer)_1737.jpg; p. 28 (bottom) https://commons.wikimedia.org/wiki/File:Charles_Messier_AGE_V10_1802.jpg; p. 29 (top inset) https://commons.wikimedia.org/wiki/File:Studio_portrait_photograph_of_Edwin_Powell_Hubble_(cropped).JPG; p. 29 (bottom inset) https://commons.wikimedia.org/wiki/File:James_E._Webb,_official_NASA_photo,_1966.jpg.

Manufactured in the United States of America

CPSIA Compliance Information: Batch #CSPK22. For Further Information contact Rosen Publishing, New York, New York at 1-800-237-9932.

CONTENTS

GALAXIES 4
SIZE IN SPACE 6
WHAT IS A GALAXY? 8
GALAXY SHAPES 12
FOCUS ON GALAXIES 14
THE BIG CRASH 18
NEBULAE 20
GALACTIC SPIN 24
BLACK HOLES 26
GALAXY SPOTTERS 28
GLOSSARY 30
FOR MORE INFORMATION 31
INDEX 32

GALAXIES

Galaxies are sculpted by gravity into gigantic shapes and clusters. Consisting of empty space, scattered with stars and planets, they spin into infinity.

Finding out about space is difficult, mostly because it is so big. In fact, everything is so far apart in the universe that scientists invented a new way to measure the greatest distances in space. This measurement is called a light-year. One light-year equals the distance light can travel in one year, about 5.88 trillion miles (9.46 trillion km).

DID YOU KNOW?

There may be 100 billion galaxies in the universe! Earth is found in a galaxy called the Milky Way. It looks like a milky streak or band of light that can be seen stretching across the night sky. The Milky Way is light-years away from any other galaxy!

SIZE IN SPACE

GIANT FACTS

- A light-year is the distance light travels in one year. Our nearest star, Alpha Centauri, is more than 4 light-years from Earth.
- It would take 200,000 years at the speed of light to cross our galaxy, the Milky Way.
- Although the planets would fit between Earth and the moon, they're actually very close to each other by universal standards!
- Scientists think our universe may be infinite, which means it might go on forever.

Alpha Centauri

Hubble Space Telescope

DID YOU KNOW?

The observable universe that scientists can see with telescopes, like the Hubble Space Telescope, is 13.8 billion light-years away from planet Earth.

WHAT IS A GALAXY?

Galaxies are great gatherings of stars and clouds of space dust, swirling across space. They are made of trillions of stars held together by gravity and strange, mysterious stuff called dark matter. In the middle of almost every galaxy is a vortex of gravity called a supermassive black hole.

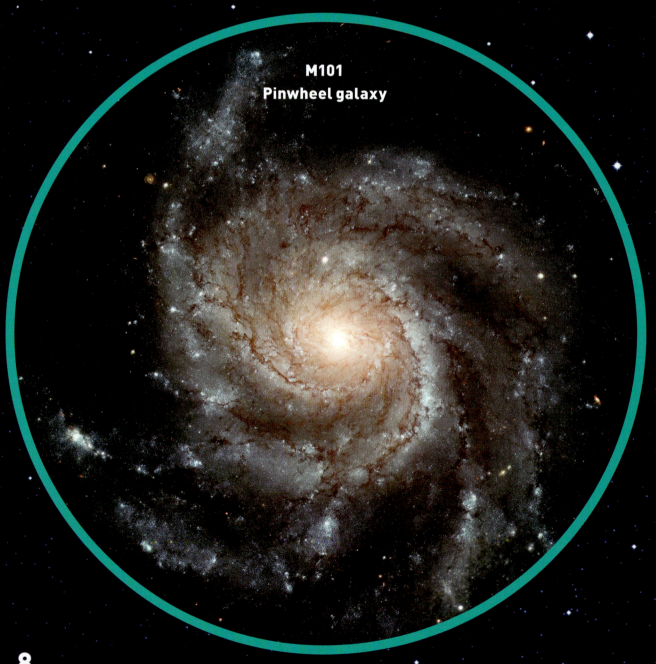

**M101
Pinwheel galaxy**

HOW MANY?

Of course, nobody really knows how many galaxies there are, but giant telescopes are always seeking to discover more. Some galaxies are found in pairs, some in clusters, and others gather in superclusters. Galaxies don't have edges, and are constantly spinning and moving across space. Sizes of galaxies and the distances they travel are almost impossible to imagine and even more difficult to measure.

EMPTY SPACES

Between the stars there is plenty of empty space, with floating clouds of dust and gas where new stars are born. Around these new stars, dust spins and clumps into planets, asteroids, meteorites, and comets, all hurled around by gravity.

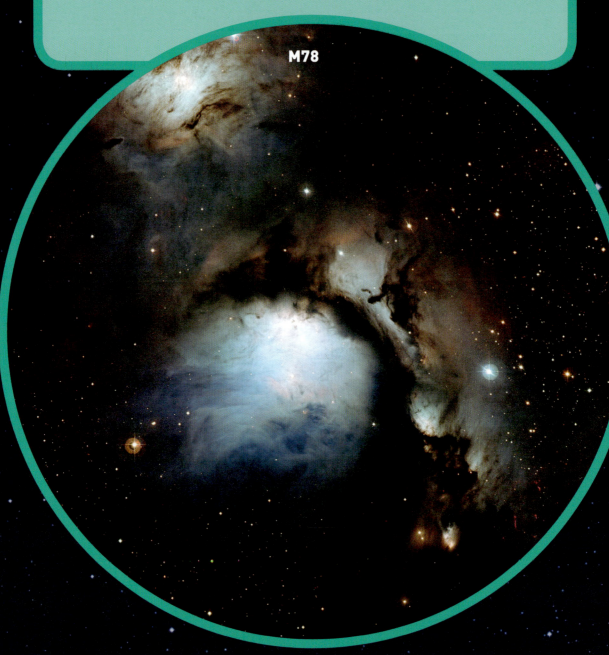

M78

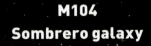

M104
Sombrero galaxy

THE "M" IN GALAXY NAMING

Galaxies are named with the letter M and a number after a French astronomer named Charles Messier (1730–1817). He published a catalog of 110 objects in space that can be seen from the Northern Hemisphere. They are named and numbered after him, using the M of his name; 42 of them are galaxies.

GALAXY SHAPES

Galaxies spin in lots of shapes, but most are spiral, barred, or elliptical. Others are shapeless blurs of stars. Our galaxy is called the Milky Way. A closer look at our milky blur shows its spiral shape, with a flat spinning disc in the middle and arches of stars curving outward into space.

Elliptical

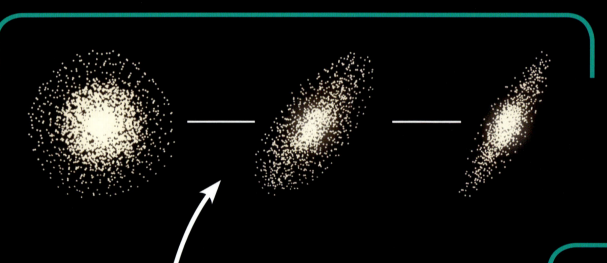

Elliptical galaxies

Largely composed of older mature stars, these types seldom have star-forming areas.

Spiral galaxies

Spiral galaxies are one of the most familiar galaxy shapes. In fact, when most people think of a galaxy, this type of galaxy shape is the first to come to mind.

Spiral

Irregular galaxies

These galaxies are often small and don't have enough gravitational force to organize into a more regular form.

Irregular

Barred spiral

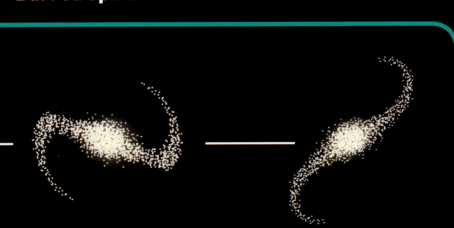

FOCUS ON GALAXIES

THE MILKY WAY: OUR GALAXY

- The Milky Way is a spiral galaxy.
- It consists of more than 100 billion stars.
- It contains our solar system, far out on a cosmic arm, 25,000 light-years from the central black hole.
- More than half of the stars are older than our 4.5-billion-year-old sun.
- Most of the galaxy looks blue, with a red center.

Milky Way

Andromeda

ANDROMEDA: A SPIRAL GALAXY

> Andromeda (M31) is a spiral galaxy.
> It is a giant galaxy, much bigger than the Milky Way, containing a trillion stars.
> It is the closest galaxy to our own Milky Way, 2.5 million light-years from Earth.

M49: AN ELLIPTICAL GALAXY

> This was the first galaxy discovered by Charles Messier in 1777.
> Elliptical galaxies spin slower and have a stretched-out circle shape. They appear red, the color of the older stars.
> There are no cold clouds of gas where new stars can form.
> It's in the Virgo group of stars.

M49

M95

M95: A BARRED GALAXY

> This galaxy has a stretched spiral shape with spinning arms at each end of a bar.
> It is 33 million light-years away.
> It sparkles with the light of young blue stars.
> It belongs to the Leo group of stars.

THE BIG CRASH

The universe is expanding, so galaxies are moving outward toward infinity. The further away they are, the faster they are moving. They often collide, in which case they either just pass through each other (because there's so much empty space) or they crash and form a giant galactic merger.

THE BIG SMASH

Andromeda and the Milky Way are moving toward each other at almost 250 miles (400 km) per hour. In about 4 billion years, the two galaxies will crash. The timing of this collision has been predicted by Europe's Gaia spacecraft. No one knows what kind of crash it will be. It's sure to light up the night sky for any life on Earth that is around to watch!

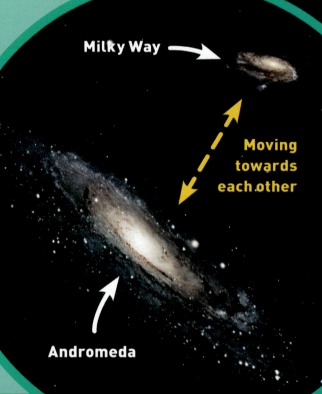

Milky Way

Moving towards each other

Andromeda

CRASHES...

Long before the Andromeda and Milky Way crash, there may be another galactic merger: the Milky Way will collide with its neighboring galaxy, the Large Magellanic Cloud, in about 2.5 billion years. This violent collision will be far from Earth and it's unlikely that our planet will feel the impact.

Large Magellanic Cloud

Milky Way

... AND COLLISIONS

The collision between the Antennae galaxies, which are located about 62 million light-years from Earth, began more than 100 million years ago and is still occurring. During the merger, 100 trillion suns' worth of material is colliding, mixing, and igniting. These two galaxies, each 100,000 light-years across, host hundreds of billions of stars.

Antennae galaxies

NEBULAE

The spaces between the stars, where dust and gas gather, are called nebulae. These gigantic masses of color form cosmic shapes that scientists can recognize and name. They glitter and glow in bright blue and red gas. Some in deep space have been photographed by the Hubble Space Telescope and the Spitzer Space Telescope.

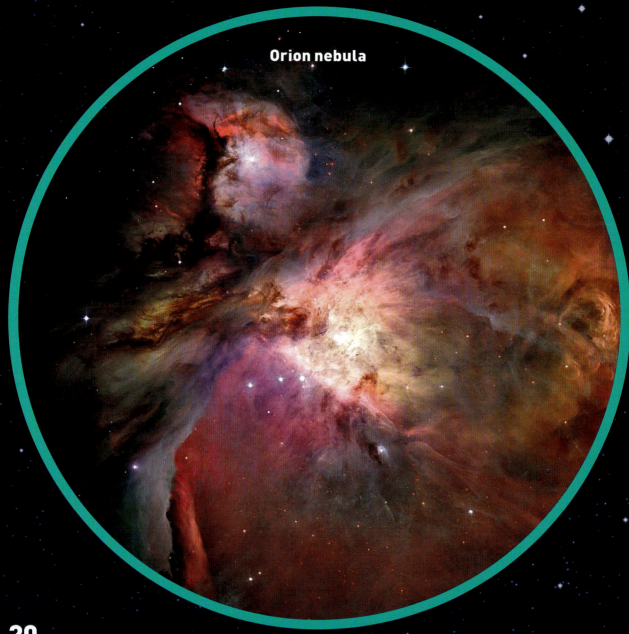

Orion nebula

Carina nebula

SPACE FOR BIRTH AND DEATH

Some nebulae are places where new stars are born, in which case they are called "star nurseries." Other nebulae form when giant stars go supernova. That is when they explode and die. The Carina Nebula is 8,500 light-years away from Earth.

Crab Nebula

This is what remains of a supernova in the constellation of Taurus. It is 6,500 light-years from Earth. A rapidly spinning neutron star is embedded in the center of the Crab Nebula.

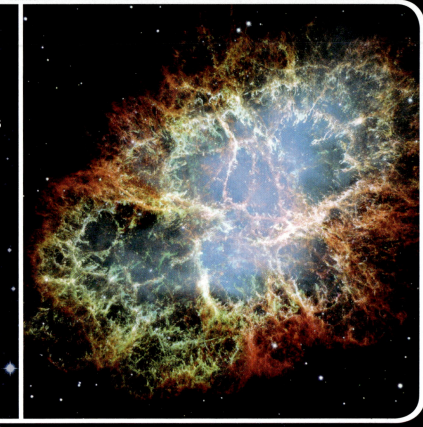

Horsehead Nebula

It's 1,500 light-years from Earth. Bright spots in the Horsehead Nebula's base are young stars just in the process of forming.

Eagle Nebula

It's 7,000 light-years from Earth. There is an active star-forming region within the nebula, known as the Pillars of Creation, which contains proto-stars.

Butterfly Nebula

This is a nebula 4,000 light-years from Earth. The bright clusters and nebulae of our night sky are often given names from nature.

GALACTIC SPIN

Like all galaxies, the Milky Way is always spinning, and we are spinning with it. Scientists have discovered that all galaxies, whatever size they are, spin a full turn once every billion years. If galaxies didn't spin, they would collapse inward into the supermassive black holes in the middle.

Here we are

The Milky Way is our home galaxy in the universe and home to 400 billion stars as well as our own sun and solar system. Our solar system is far out on the Orion Spur of the spiral-shaped Milky Way galaxy. The Milky Way, along with everything else in the universe, is moving through space. Earth moves around the sun, and the sun moves around the Milky Way,

120,000–180,000 light-years in diameter

Sun

Orion Spur

Perseus arm

Outer arm

DID YOU KNOW?

We don't have a picture of the entire Milky Way, as we are inside it. The galactic disc is about 26,000 light-years from the galactic center. It would be like trying to take a picture of your own house from the inside!

Supermassive black hole called Sagittarius A*

DIRECTION OF SPIN

Milky Way spin

Our galaxy spins really slowly. It takes about 220 million years for our solar system to make a complete orbit of the Milky Way, so one galactic turn ago, dinosaurs roamed Earth. There have only been 20 galactic turns of the Milky Way since our solar system was formed. The gas and dust in our galaxy is rotating at around 168 miles (270 km) per second.

BLACK HOLES

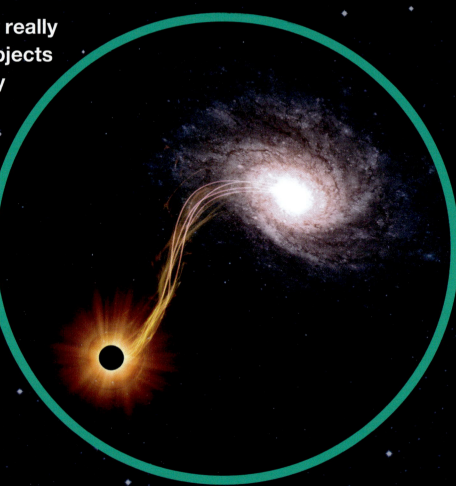

Black holes are not really holes. They are objects in space where gravity is so strong that even light gets bent and sucked in. Space telescopes show what happens to light and stars around a black hole, so we know they are out there. Nothing can ever escape from a black hole.

DID YOU KNOW?

If you were to fall into a black hole (which you won't), you would be "spaghettified." This means that the forces of gravity in the black hole would stretch you out into thin, spaghetti-like strips!

BLACK HOLE FACTS

- Some black holes formed after the Big Bang and others form when stars die.
- There are black holes of many different sizes all over the universe.
- All galaxies swirl around a black hole, some of which are supermassive.
- The supermassive black hole at the center of the Milky Way galaxy is called Sagittarius A*.

ON CAMERA

In an exciting scientific breakthrough, a black hole was photographed for the first time in 2019. It is a black hole that is 55 million light-years away from Earth and is at the center of a galaxy called M87.

GALAXY SPOTTERS

THOMAS WRIGHT

(1711–1786)
An Englishman who first described the Milky Way. He realized that Earth (and humans on Earth) are tiny relative to the scale of a vast universe.

CHARLES MESSIER

(1730–1817)
A French astronomer who made a list of 110 blurry light objects in the sky. He made the list because he wanted to tell the difference between comets and these other objects, which were clusters of stars and nebulae.

EDWIN HUBBLE

(1889–1953)
An American who discovered a way of grouping galaxies and figured out that the universe is expanding. The Hubble Space Telescope named after him is about the size of a school bus. It takes pictures of stars and galaxies in deep space.

JAMES WEBB

(1906–1992)
An American who ran the American space agency NASA and after whom the new James Webb Space Telescope is named.

James Webb Space Telescope

GLOSSARY

astronomer a scientist who studies space
collide the hitting of two objects against one another
diameter the distance from one side of a round object to another through its center
elliptical shaped like a flattened circle
gravity the force that pulls objects toward the center of a planet or star
ignite to set on fire
infinity having no limits or end
observable able to be seen
orbit to travel in a circle or oval around something, or the path used to make that trip
rotate to turn around a fixed point
solar system the sun and all the space objects that orbit it, including the planets and their moons
spiral a shape or line that curls outward from a center point
telescope a tool that makes faraway objects look bigger and closer
universe everything that exists

FOR MORE INFORMATION

BOOKS

Beer, Julie, and Stephanie Warren Drimmer. *Can't Get Enough Space Stuff.* Washington, DC: National Geographic, 2022.

Light, Charlie. *To The Milky Way and Beyond: Explorations Outside the Solar System*. Gareth Stevens Publishing, 2021.

Nargi, Lela. *Mysteries of Planets, Stars, and Galaxies*. North Mankato, MN: Capstone Press, 2021.

WEBSITES

www.ducksters.com/science/galaxies.php
Find out even more fun facts about galaxies!

kids.nationalgeographic.com/space/article/milky-way
Learn more about the Milky Way here.

spaceplace.nasa.gov
Check out NASA's website for kids.

Publisher's note to educators and parents: Our editors have carefully reviewed these websites to ensure that they are suitable for students. Many websites change frequently, however, and we cannot guarantee that a site's future contents will continue to meet our high standards of quality and educational value. Be advised that students should be closely supervised whenever they access the internet.

INDEX

Alpha Centauri 6
Andromeda 15, 18, 19
barred spiral galaxy 12, 13, 17
black hole 8, 14, 24, 26, 27
comets 10, 28
Earth 4, 5, 6, 7, 15, 22, 23, 24, 25, 27, 28
elliptical galaxy 12, 16
Hubble, Edwin 29
Hubble Space Telescope 7, 20, 29
irregular galaxy 13
James Webb Space Telescope 29
light-year 4, 5, 6, 7, 14, 15, 17, 19, 21, 22, 23, 25, 27

Messier, Charles 11, 16, 28
M49 16
Milky Way 5, 6, 12, 14, 15, 18, 19, 24, 25, 27, 28
M95 17
planets 10
Sagittarius A* 27
spiral galaxy 12, 13, 14, 15, 24
Spitzer Space Telescope 20
stars 4, 6, 10, 12, 14, 15, 16, 17, 19, 20, 21, 22, 23, 25, 28, 29
sun 14, 24
supernova 21, 22
Webb, James 29
Wright, Thomas 28